Mantra Publishing Limited
5 Alexandra Grove, London N12 8NU

The Night The Animals Fought

by Jesus Zaton
Illustrated by Jesus Gaban

MANTRA

It was a dry summer.
There was hardly any food.
Only a few plants and the odd bush remained.
All the animals went hungry.

The buffalo walked for miles looking for food,
but he could find nothing to eat.
As the sun set behind the mountains he turned
towards home, tired and weak with hunger.

He passed the only pond which hadn't yet dried up, and stopped to have a drink.
Suddenly he noticed a shining round object floating in the clear water.
"Food at last!" cried the buffalo eagerly and was just about to grab it when he heard a mighty growl.

"Hey! What brings you here at this late hour?" roared a fierce lion. Even though he was much thinner now, the lion still made the buffalo tremble with fear.

"I've dropped this thing in the water," said the buffalo," and I am trying to get it back."

"This is my pond," growled the lion. "Everything on it belongs to me."

"No it doesn't," replied the buffalo bravely and the two began to quarrel.

The angry sounds awoke all the other animals. They gathered round the pond. Some were curious, and others thought they could have some fun.

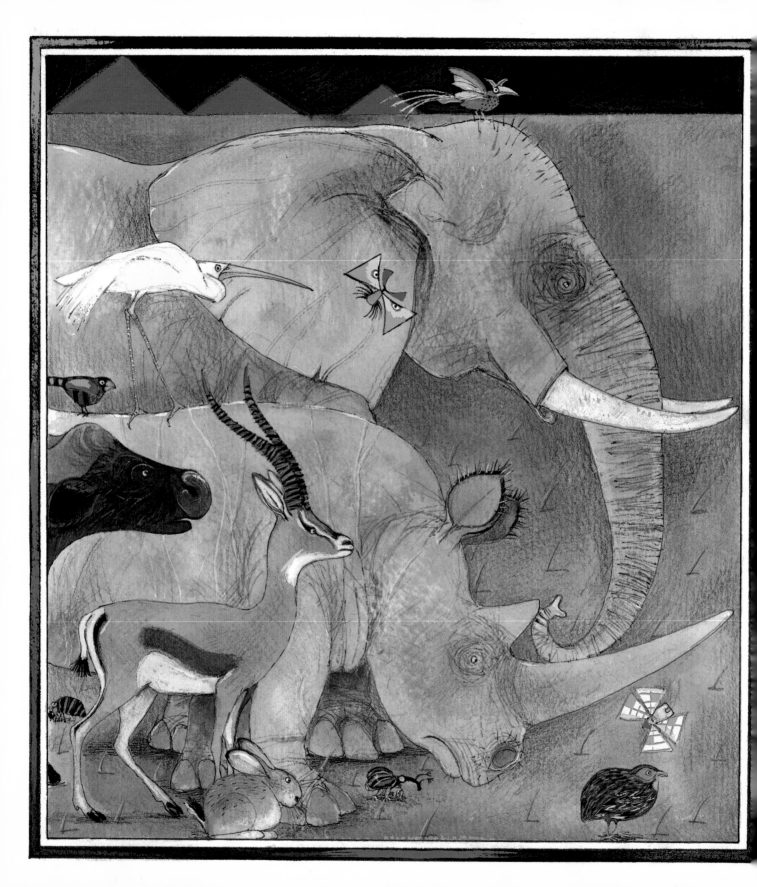

Soon they began to take sides.
The gazelle, the rhino, the rabbit and the elephant disliked the lion. They joined with the buffalo, shouting, "Finders, keepers."
The cheetah, the mouse, the snake and the jackal thought the lion would surely win. They took his side, yelling, "Mine, mine, mine."

Meanwhile, a large and greedy vulture watched all that was happening. "If there isn't a fight I'll get nothing to eat," he thought, so he called out loudly, "May the strongest win!"

The proud lion and the foolish buffalo agreed immediately. The lion roared with rage and the buffalo bellowed back angrily.

Then, the fight began.

Soon, all the animals started fighting one another and the noise was deafening.

The battle lasted all night. Then, just at dawn, a little squirrel ran up to the lion and the buffalo. She said, "Why don't you share the shining object in the pond?" "What a good idea," said the badly bruised buffalo. " I quite agree," said the tired lion licking his wounds.

All the animals ran to the pond.
There, right in the middle, was the shining round object.

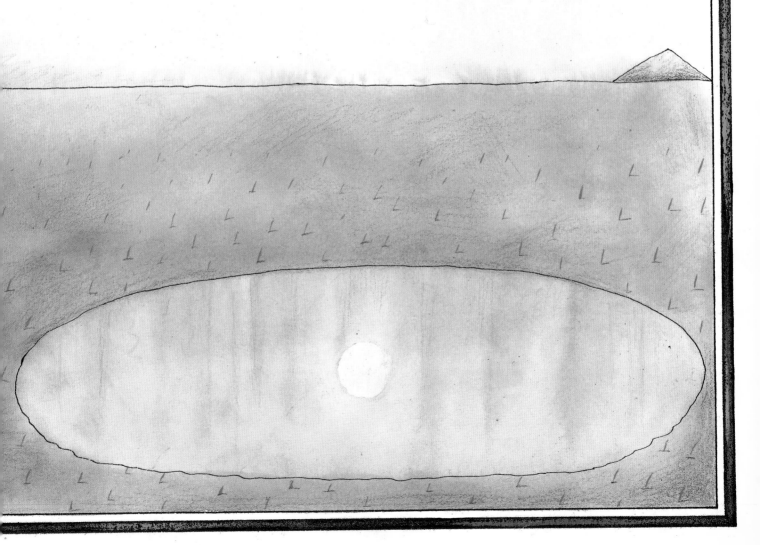

Then a strange thing happened.
The sun came out from behind the mountains and
the shining object faded slowly away.
It had been only a reflection of the moon.
"Is *this* what we have been fighting for?" thought the
animals, feeling very foolish.
They walked away slowly... their heads bowed in
shame.